BURNING
BLUE

NEW LOVERS is a series devoted to
publishing new works of erotica
that explore the complexities
bedevilling contemporary
life, culture, and
art today.

OTHER TITLES IN THE SERIES

BURNING
BLUE

×

CARA BENEDETTO

BADLANDS UNLIMITED
NEW LOVERS
N°6

Burning Blue
by Cara Benedetto

New Lovers No.6

Published by:
Badlands Unlimited LLC
P.O. Box 320310
Brooklyn, NY 11232
Tel: +1 718 788 6668
operator@badlandsunlimited.com
www.badlandsunlimited.com

Series editors: Paul Chan, Ian Cheng, Micaela Durand, Matthew So
Copy editor: Charlotte Carter
Editorial assistant: Angela Brown
Ebook designer: Ian Cheng
Front cover design by Kobi Benzari
Endpaper and interior art by Mira Dancy
Special thanks to Luke Brown, Elisa Leshowitz, Marlo Poras

Paper book distributed in the Americas by:
ARTBOOK | D.A.P. USA
155 6th Avenue, 2nd Floor
New York, NY 10013
Tel. +1 800 338 BOOK
www.artbook.com

Paper book distributed in Europe by:
Buchhandlung Walther König
Ehrenstrasse 4
50672 Köln
www.buchhandlung-walther-koenig.de

Printed in the United States of America

ISBN: 978-1-936440-84-9
E-Book ISBN: 978-1-936440-85-6

www.badlandsunlimited.com

For Cammi

CONTENTS

Part One
Blood Let

The woman's thighs were heavy and wet.

She was slick with arousal and had grown used to changing her panties often and daily. As she boarded the train she felt moisture move between legs.

Settling into a window seat, the woman watched her reflection flicker with the train car's fluorescent lights. The car was half empty and smelled of her musty lilac scent. In haste she'd forgotten pads. *Screw it*, she thought. *Tonight I'll bleed freely*. Her jeans turned maroon as the air moved around her in strange hormonal waves. She was grateful there were no cramps tonight.

The conductor gave her a familiar wink as she stepped onto the deserted platform. Like a classic noir opening shot, the taxi pulled up out of darkness and delivered her, in silence, to the secluded cabin. As the cab's taillights disappeared behind a thick forest line, she felt herself relaxing. Josey smiled to herself when she realized that she felt more normal in a place as alien and strange as her own body had become.

She made her way up the steps and stumbled through the dimly lit screened-in porch. The front door was unlocked. Swiping the wall, she hit a switch. Four large barn lights lit a pretty oak table to seat six, a modest kitchen, and a casual living room set. All in one pretty 'A' frame room.

She didn't bother to unpack her bag. There wasn't much: underwear, wool socks, a makeup bag, two scratch-offs, her favorite Malbec, and a few boxes of coconut water.

She threw her belongings onto a wicker chair and began to undress. She felt the need to get away from herself. Making her way to the bathroom, she wrenched her jeans over sticky legs and ran a hot bath.

Her panic was gone. She dug up a wine glass and, Malbec in tow, eased her way into the boiling water, turning the foam bath into a similar shade of rose.

Josey closed her eyes as the hot water seeped into her organs. She was a frog with porous skin, gulping air in quiet chirps. She went over the long day that had led her there.

"There's not enough blue," he'd said flatly. Earlier that afternoon she had watched the squat man, her gallerist, hover over her paintings like a giant black fly. True to a fly's character, the direction of his buzz was erratic and influenced by the smell of blood. "There's just *too* much red." She swatted his complaint with an eyeroll. The mention of red reminded her of the growing wet spot between her legs.

Every night that month Josey had woken to cramping, her upper thighs painted in a light wash of blood. She didn't know why she was bleeding but had some guesses. As far as she was concerned it was like anybody's critical moments in life. Josey would evade the issue. Just like the first time she had sex. When the guy asked if she was okay, pointing to the blood on the sheets, she acted as if she didn't know what he was talking about. Just like before, she would ignore the blood and tell no one, not even her husband. She let herself bleed into a deep red secret.

"I like it red. It's violent." She said this in a near whisper while gazing out the gallery window. When she finally turned to look at him, she found an apathetic face. She quickly looked away, tossing her long white hair behind her. "Anyways, my paintings can't always match your wardrobe, Hans. If you want I can get you a bowtie with hearts." Her gallerist grimaced and returned his half focus to the painting.

Josey loved her paintings, she had made them, after all, but there were times when she witnessed people staring at them and she didn't know what they saw. She was even a little confused as to where their admiration came from, and it made her uncomfortable to have a stranger's eyes twitching all over her decisions. With a few words she politely exited the gallery and walked out into the glaring

Manhattan neighborhood of Chelsea.

An ex-model, Josey knew what it felt like to be adored and she never wanted it to stop. She was only forty-five but already she felt the coming of invisibility. She missed the grease stains men left with their lingering looks. She missed the eyes of envy cast by other women who would never look as good in a halter top and cut-offs.

Even when she'd had the wherewithal to refer to such harassment as a product of Rape Culture, she enjoyed having the power to acknowledge, or ignore, the attention. Now that age was catching on and in between her legs, she felt a new kind of lack. She felt absent. She needed to match the remove she felt.

Josey needed a break from the everyday.

She called her husband Asher to let him know she was leaving town. Even though they slept in the same bed every night, they hadn't spoken in days. As usual, he was without affect. She stopped by her friend Ryan's to pick up the keys, and then headed upstate, to bleed in peace.

×

The gentleness of the next two weeks slowed down her body clock. Josey bled while wandering through books, beach, and forest, and kept on bleeding. Sometimes she dripped onto the hardwood floor and imagined that the flecks would bubble up into a soft, wormy head, a character from her favorite horror film, *Hellraiser*.

She figured that in this way she could still procreate. Through her slow drippings on the floor she would build a monster and name it Lise, after the vengeful astronaut. Lise was infamous for wearing a NASA diaper to save time as she drove across the country on her way to kidnap the girlfriend of her ex-lover. Josey thought Lise was cool, in a desperate kind of way.

Josey let her mind wander and rest, fill up with fantasies instead of anxieties. Josey had become increasingly horny over the last few months. She not only eyeballed both men and women, but now teenagers were viable options. She felt a kinship with them because of the uncontrollable and insatiable desire she knew they must also experience. She had even begun to strike up flirtations with strangers, which she'd never dared before. It was exciting to see people's eyes move over her, taking her in as if she could still be attractive, with a little effort.

Josey had never considered herself needy, vain, or shallow, but now that she couldn't reinforce the population, she felt as though she had lost a kind of value. She had lost the ability to make a soldier, a slave, or a king. She had lost their game. Josey knew that her remaining worth was fleeting and that she'd have to figure out a new set of values before everyone found her out. She hunted around for some hidden or forgotten talents and came up with a mental list:

1. Drawing lopsided self-portraits

2. Making cats feel good about themselves

3. Sexting

Not bad, she thought. In that moment she had the irrational idea that she might very well bleed until she died, and she was okay with that. She had to be. She would let the walls dissolve on their own terms.

The following day was hot. Josey had woken early, to clear periwinkle skies and a desire to run. Flat feet punched the ground as she ran, grinding her flesh into her hipbone sockets. She didn't care that it would culminate in pain. She wanted to feel her body. Perhaps she simply wanted to feel.

She decided to run to Antler's General Store, a local market that doubled as a café. Josey was cooling herself with a tall iced mocha, sipping from a green straw and sweating onto a *New York Times*, when she noticed a young woman seated in the corner.

The woman had lengthy bare legs that sprawled haphazardly from under the small table. Her long torso steadied toned arms that hovered over a sleek black laptop. She was in deep concentration, unaware of even her own body.

Her total absorption in the screen allowed Josey to indulge a gaze. She was entranced by the woman's soft, dark skin and assured movements. Her eyes wandered slowly over the girl's perfect breasts, barely concealed by a loose black tank. The girl's mouth parted slightly as she inhaled the blue abyss in front of her.

Dark hair, shaved on one side, rolled out in cascades over smooth shoulder blades. Her body was taut and perspiring, wet and unaware of the heat she exuded. She was raw sex removed. Josey thought the girl looked like an emotionless island that Josey could catch her breath on.

A waft of her own intense body odor reminded Josey that she was a sweaty mess. She tore herself away from the scene and hit the path, stabbing the ground with the fullness of a flat-footed stride. As she ran, strokes of lightning lit up her brain in flashes of pain, but Josey showed no sign of suffering. For once her thoughts were elsewhere.

Josey went back to the café at the same time the next day and found the girl in the exact same pose. Taking a closer seat, Josey caught a glimpse of the girl's computer screen. She seemed to be watching what looked like sex.

Flashes of flesh streaked the screen in golden and black hues. The camera closed in on a sultry middle-aged brunette. She was on all fours, breasts hanging loosely. She opened her mouth wide as a spurt of come shot onto her glossy pink lips. A hot blonde boy with a big muscly body like a surfer's was jerking himself off onto the faces and bodies of several older women. *It's like an assembly or receiving line.* Josey laughed at the comparison, thinking back to her own wedding and how the rice being thrown at her felt the same.

This young woman looks so alive,

Josey thought. Watching porn in public was brave. Josey couldn't help but feel vulnerable and high in the girl's presence.

"I'm Josey. What's your name?"

"Uh," she said, not looking up, "name's Trish." The woman was absorbed by what she was watching, and every once in a while, clicking on.

"Looks like you're pretty busy… but… maybe not as busy as them." Josey pointed to the computer, where the screen now held one of the women being throttled from behind as the other women licked the surfer's glistening torso. Josey imagined the storyline had something to do with a Mothers Against Drunk Driving meeting gone good. "Mind if I watch?" she asked, peeking over Trish's shoulder, showing the slightest sliver of a smile.

Finally looking Josey squarely in the face, Trish removed her headphones, almost smiling, and replied, "Sure, if that's what you're into." And then, "Is there something you'd rather watch?"

Josey smiled. "I thought you'd never ask. Do you have anything with older women, heels…and uh…blood?"

This was the second time Trish almost smiled. "Yes, I have stuff with older women and heels…but blood, really?"

"Yeah, I'm into blood. And older women. Big deal." Josey shrugged her shoulders and tried to sound as New York City cool as she could.

"Well. It'll take some time. I gotta run. Let's meet tomorrow. Same time, same place."

"K," Josey accepted the dare, "looking forward to it."

×

Josey had become aroused by the fleshy footage and decided to hit Fish Lipps, a local bar just down the road. There were two bands playing that night: *The Hearty Hearts,* a three-person act that dominated the interior; and *Our Ladies of the Shore*, two yodeling hippies on a straw stage in the tiki tent out back.

She opted for inside and sat at the bar. She knew there'd be some random trouble, what with the empty stool next to her. She waited. A wrinkly gentleman in his late 60s bought her a rose from a vendor. She chose yellow. Next in line was a self-proclaimed Solver of Problems named Keith. He smelled like horseshit on pizza and Josey refused to let him pay for her Corona. Third was Jesse, a half-wit rich kid who hadn't remembered his name for four days because of an excessive intake of mushrooms.

Of the three, Jesse was the most entertaining, and she let him talk about himself endlessly while she imagined sucking on the fingers of Brenda, the big-hipped bartender. All the while Josey bled on the stool, conjuring Lise the Astronaut and her fight against cheating boyfriends and boring husbands that laid claim to her Planet Ear.

Asher called at some point and they

chatted about nothing. When he said he missed her, she became strangely impatient. She childishly pretended the line was cut, and hung up on him. She was tipsy, but in that moment Josey felt far away from her husband. She'd never contemplated cheating on Asher before, but it seemed beyond her control now. Her body was making the decisions.

As last call approached, Jesse drunkenly demanded that everyone go swimming. Josey was planning her escape when she noticed a shorter man behind Jesse. He seemed strong, with half-hidden bicep tattoos and an ethereal logic to his manners. Josey took stock and pretended not to be listening as she walked up and waved a quick and unnecessary goodbye to Jesse. His friend didn't notice her but Jesse did, and immediately went on a tirade about how they all needed to go swimming, or do a shot, in that instant.

In a joint effort to appease an increasingly belligerent Jesse, Josey and Jesse's tattooed friend, Mark, agreed to a tequila shot and a quick dip. Josey quickly introduced herself, and together the unlikely threesome trotted to the shore and stripped.

The air was frigid. The water slapped their skins and each howled and yelped in turn. As they shared a few laughs Josey caught Mark looking at her ass. Jesse paraded his nakedness, while Mark seemed tense with apprehension. Josey wore nothing at all and didn't think twice about the blood. She imagined herself to be a thin and wounded shark hovering over its prey in the dark. A deep-sea demon hoping to kill before bleeding to death.

Josey dove deep. Swept up by a sudden wave, she landed directly in Mark's lap. She wrapped an arm around his waist, locking herself into his side. He acted mildly surprised but didn't protest. She pulled him closer and whispered into his ear, "Are we drowning?"

With a sly smile Mark shed his timid demeanor and whispered back, "By the time I'm done with you, you'll wish we were."

They quickly got into a rough rhythm. The pulsing sea synchronized his growing erection against her salty pearl. She guided his hand into her swollen lips and swallowed his chilly fingertips. He uttered a low moan, fingering her deep and wet spaces.

He grasped inside her shark jaw, holding her against the waves, becoming more and more excited. His mouth wore itself out on her erect nipples. Josey loved having her breasts sucked and beaten by a man's teeth. He gnawed on her neck with one hand inside her warm and muscled pussy while the freezing water licked at her bloody body.

Against the waves, he lifted her hips and thrust his cock inside her, burying it to the base. She kissed his mouth tenderly as he yanked at her insides, rocking back and forth with the waves. They wore the dark water like a blanket.

"Harder," she whispered into his ear. "Make me feel again."

He stopped plunging for a moment to catch her eye. She was begging.

"Kill me with your cock," she said in a flat and earnest tone.

Her words excited him; he wanted to please her, even if that meant breaking her beautiful body in two. He shifted to hold her back with both forearms. Clutching her close, he pushed in deep. He throttled and pumped. Her head fell back as words he didn't understand fell out of her throat.

The underwater dance felt good between them. They agreed on the terms that the sand carried to each of their most private and pretty parts. There was no hurry and they took time weeding the sea out from the spaces that separated them from one another.

Jesse got pushed around by the water and eventually passed out on the shore. Thirty minutes later he woke to the steamy scene unfolding before him. Mark held Josey's ass just above sea level. Jesse, in his drunken stupor, shouted in awe that the moon was getting fucked.

Jesse stroked his own growing erection as he watched, then staggered into the water, positioning himself behind Josey's moon. He rubbed his cock against her cold cheeks, promising, "I'm going to fuck you harder than him." She grasped his hard-on behind her, and slipped herself on top of him. He violently thrust his cock into her aching ass. Jesse let out a low growl, rocking back and forth with the waves, using Mark's body as leverage. Mark grasped at Josey's hips and breasts. She held them both between her thighs.

They took turns kissing her long neck. The men were barnacles on the side of her lean shark body. Together their desire wept over her and the three submerged their heat into the cool water. A darkly lit moon hung in a blood-colored sky.

×

Josey left that night nameless. She had left no child behind. There was no one in an empty world, a thicket of seaweed among lost eggs. When she returned home she drank three big glasses of water and readied for her date on the screen side of life the very next day. Trish was on her mind as she got into bed and left planet Earth.

×

"What time is it? I'm not ready yet." Trish snapped as Josey moved towards her table. Josey was desperately hungover. Grunting a low growl, she fell into the chair beside Trish. Josey sat still in an effort to stop the spinning.

Trish didn't notice and continued to prepare. Josey closed her eyes and breathed deeply. When she opened them she realized that she was no longer spinning, the fog was beginning to clear. *Was it possible that the presence of this odd, abrasive girl was helping her hangover?*

She watched Trish shuffle papers from her backpack to remove a clunky PC. "Find anything good?" Josey asked. Trish turned to give her a smirk that broadened into a 'you bet your ass I did' smile. In that moment Josey noticed how pretty Trish was, with high cheekbones and a direct gaze. She wore a half shirt that revealed her elegant square shoulders and deep shades of sunkissed skin.

As Trish waited for her computer to warm up, she lightly touched Josey's taxi-yellow nail polish. Josey blushed at the touch. She felt a wave of heat move through her arms. By the time she could say anything, Trish had placed a headset over Josey's ears and hit Play.

A ray of sunlight hit the backlit screen. Josey had to squint to see beyond their reflections. There were two women on a bed, creating a horizontal human 'T'. A thin and quick-bodied girl hovered over and licked the protruding nipples of a pretty, buxom blonde. Soft moans emanated from the headset. The women moved in rhythm to one another's sound. The pretty bottom, who was much older, was getting louder, but the darting young woman on top, rubbing her into being, was the clear aggressor.

The top wore a black silk demi bra barely covering her black nipples, and red stilettos, as she fisted and sucked at the voluptuous bottom. The receiver wore nothing but white knee-high stockings.

Josey was entranced with the scene. Just before Trish turned up the screen's brightness Josey caught Trish's eye in the reflection. Together they watched with shallow breath.

After what seemed to be hours Josey noticed that the two women had slowed down to a snail's pace and then performed cunnilingus and kisses in reverse. Until then she hadn't noticed Trish's middle finger tapping a small mouse. Trish had been adjusting the speed and movement of the film the entire time. She seemed to do it live and in accordance with the erotics. Josey's tight black jeans began to press into her rapidly swelling clit as Trish continued to tap, controlling the scene. She pretended not to notice and kept her eyes on the laptop. She was afraid that if she made eye contact with Trish her arousal would be found out.

Trish seemed oblivious to Josey and continued tapping. Josey thought she heard clicking sounds coming from Trish's tongue but was unsure because of the increasingly noisy sex happening on screen. Her body began to ooze and she knew it was more blood mixed with something left over from the previous night. Or maybe, she thought to herself, it was something new.

Trish brought down the screen with a loud snap. The scene had ended with the two women coming into one another's open mouth. Josey had become wet and squeezed her taut thighs together. She was unsure if Trish could smell her new juices. "What'd ya think?" the younger woman asked.

Josey met her eyes for an instant before her cheeks flushed red and she responded in a soft exhale, "I liked it, thanks."

"Same time, same place tomorrow? Turns out I've got a lot of this stuff." This time Trish was looking away. Josey thought she noticed a slight indentation in her cheek, as if Trish was chewing the inside of her mouth.

"Sure, I'm game. I'm driving towards town. Do you need a ride somewhere?" she asked, doing her best to sound casual.

"Uh, no thanks, I'm good. See ya tomorrow." With that, Trish briskly stood up and strode out without looking back.

She walked with a stiff neck, while the rest of her body seemed loose and aloof, as if she was compensating for an injury of some kind. *Funny girl*, Josey thought to herself. She reached across the table, intending to return the coffee cups to the counter, but realized, smiling to herself, that neither of them had ordered coffee. She waved to the girl at the counter and moved hurriedly towards the door.

As she exited the cafe she let her mind drift over the sundrenched scene. They certainly made an odd pair. A pretty, abrasive punk and a desperate middle-aged professional sitting next to each other watching pre-lunchtime porn. Josey was aroused, and it wasn't just because of the porn. Her engorged clit rubbed against the crotch of her jeans. She ached to get out of them to release that stubborn feeling.

Josey laid down on her stomach in the backseat of her car. Pressing palm and fist into her vulva, she worked rapidly to pronounce her desire, nearly whimpering as she came hard twice. Her heavy breathing slowed to mime the rhythm of the women, controlled by the fervent twitch of Trish's tapping fingers as she clicked out a tongue to clit ratio. Josey moaned furiously in time with her wet blood-pain and new want.

When she arrived at the cabin there was a white truck parked to the side of the driveway. The back gate creaked ajar. Josey quietly sneaked around the edge of the cabin. Peeking over the fence she found a young man with a mop of black hair that fell onto bare broad shoulders. She announced herself with a wave and moved closer. She wondered if her blood and recent come were scenting her in his direction.

"Oh hey, I came to clean your pool. I usually do it for Mr. Scafferd once a month."

"You're a friend of Ryan's?"

"Yeah, well, my dad is. I'm friends with his son, Maurice."

"Small world. I'm Maurice's godmother."

"Yeah? We went to language camp together last summer, but...we haven't really talked since."

"Oh? Why's that?" Josey looked him in the eye.

"Well, uh, he stole my girlfriend."

Josey smiled. She loved how open young people were. "Ah-ha. Well…there will be more." She stared into his dark eyes. "Can I offer you something?"

He smirked.

Josey ran her eyes over his strong, hairless chest before she moved through the kitchen to collect a soda and bathing suit. *How old is he?* she thought. *He looks like God.*

"Sorry, what's your name?"

"Christian. Thanks, Mrs. Monroe."

"Call me Josey. Why don't you take a break with me?"

They lay at the side of the pool sipping Cokes. Josey wore a red string bikini that pushed her breasts high and her ass out. As Christian talked her through his young lifetime achievements, Josey let her eyes play all over him. She thought he may have noticed that she was casting a line in his direction, but didn't think much of it. He was almost seventeen. He could handle it.

It was a hot day and they needed to cool down. Christian performed a cannonball, flirtatiously splashing Josey. Buffeted by her vertical dive, Josey's bikini top fell off, leaving her topless under a grateful sun. Christian smiled when he noticed. He quickly lost his grin as she stood up to face him without any hint of concern for her missing top.

He stood two strides from her. She saw him take a large gulp as she moved towards him. Josey fingered her nipple with one hand, while the other hand touched her wet lips. She sucked a finger. He watched her drip.

She moved a step closer, brushing the giant eel in the process. She took his hand and placed his middle finger directly into her hot mouth. He swallowed a few more knots in his throat and then placed his other hand on her neck. Like a clumsy child, he moved his hand down her breast, waist, and ass, bringing her closer so that their faces nearly touched. He watched and listened to her suck on his tingling fingertips.

Out of patience, Christian kissed her hard. They moved towards the edge. She turned around, facing away from him, towards the forest. He clumsily pushed a few fingers inside her from behind. She was warm and wet and clenched his fingers.

Josey pushed down with her hips, into his grip, enveloping his large teenage boy fist. The water sluiced in a sharp wave onto the grassy lawn next to the pool. He responded like a star pitcher for a high school baseball team, fucking her, a solid curve ball. "I can't wait, I need to be inside you now." She leaned forward and closed her eyes on the woods as he hurriedly pushed his trunks down.

Eager to please, he yanked at her bikini bottom, ripping the ties, and lifted her onto his engorged fresh young cock. He worked himself into her. She felt herself stretch and fold. He pushed in deep. "Oh Mrs. Monroe," he quaked, his voice nearly cracking with wonder. She begged the boy to fuck her harder, to pull her hair, as he slammed her over and over against a lake colored sky with soft tree shadows watching in cool relief.

×

Josey flipped her phone closed and ate the yogurt's berry bottom. Only an hour until she met Trish for the second installment of middle-aged lesbian porn class. She couldn't wait. Picking up her phone again she was reminded of the strange play of events from the night before.

It was still early. After Christian finished cleaning her pool she spoke with Asher briefly. He was distracted as usual. Asher had taken to drinking early in the day, so that by the time they spoke he was already half gone. She missed the long talks they used to have as they fell asleep in one another's arms, but that hadn't happened for years. Feeling even more alone after they had spoken, Josey curled up with wine by the fire, and succumbed to sleep with the sun.

Her dreams were littered with headless bodies ripping at canvas made of dark red silk. Around 3 A.M. she woke drenched in blood. For a moment she believed she'd find a decapitated head in bed but soon realized it was more of the same; eggs moving out. She cleaned up and fell asleep on the couch.

✕

"I like your nails."

Josey became excited. "I love giving

manicures. Do you want one? I have a nice periwinkle blue that would look great with your keyboard."

"I'll think about it." Trish took a long suck from her grande iced mocha topped with a ton of whipped cream. Josey liked the way Trish punctuated her words with taps and sucks.

"What are we watching today?"

Trish nearly sprang out of her seat. She was clearly nervous, and that made Josey very curious. *What excited this strange young woman who seems to have seen it all?* "I've got something weird to show you," Trish said. "Not sure you'll like it but you mentioned blood, so why not…?"

Nice, Josey thought, *she's going for it*. Josey gestured 'go ahead.' Trish hit Play. They looked into a black screen and this time directly into one another's reflected gaze.

There were several people. It looked like they were outside. It was amateur. Homemade. Josey squinted to see more clearly. The headphones were squeezing her head today. They felt tighter. The people were big and small, young and old; there were children and men watching on the side. Josey blinked. Trish bit her thumbnail.

The women were in a circle and there was something covering their limbs, *or were some of them missing limbs? No, it was dirt. Dirt as black as night.* But it seemed that some of them had to be bleeding. *Where else would all that blood be coming from?* And their faces were hard to see.

They were stuffed between the legs of one another.

Josey was reminded of *The Human Centipede*, the goriest horror film she'd ever seen, and quickly realized that it paled in comparison to what they were watching. There were sounds of muffled screams and children whimpering. The men watched somberly. The camerawork was terrible. The image jostled from side to side.

What was she looking at? She had no idea. It must be some kind of ritual. She broke character and looked at Trish with a question mark plastered on her forehead. Trish hit Pause and said, "It's called *The End of Periods*. It's a ritual." Josey smiled and motioned for her to continue.

She watched with an open face. She let the question mark wrinkles fade. Josey spent the rest of the next half hour or so thinking about her phantom children and husband watching her eat another woman out while she and the woman covered each other in menopausal blood. She felt high.

At the end, she hugged Trish and wouldn't take no for an answer. She would touch her hands and improve her beds one way or another. They agreed to meet at Josey's place later that night.

Still high, Josey had arranged a beautiful spread for Trish's manicure. She heated lavender scented oils and she bought a perfectly dry Chardonnay to go with blood oranges and pecorino, heirloom tomatoes, and beet salad.

Everything would stain red, except for Trish's new nails. Josey loved to give a good manicure.

She felt a sudden and surprising pang of anxiety. After a quick change of clothing Josey realized that she was nervous because she felt challenged by this young woman and wanted to impress her. Smiling to herself, she glanced in the mirror and wondered where the night might lead.

Trish drove in on a high-riding black Vespa. She was uncharacteristically femme, in fuchsia lipstick, eyeliner, a short jean skirt, and purple zip-up top. She looked gorgeous. "Nice place."

"Thanks, it's not mine. Care for wine?"

Trish wandered over to the bookshelf

and started picking through the limited collection. She seemed fairly uninterested, but buzzed with an extraordinary energy. Josey couldn't tell what was going on in the young girl's mind. She turned her back to her to finish cutting beets. After a moment of silence, Trish said, "I hope you liked the film."

Relieved it wasn't a question, Josey didn't turn around. "I loved it," she said, sucking her stomach in lightly.

Another moment of silence and then Josey felt a cool hand on the back of her neck. "You look sunburned. Are you using protection?" Josey flushed pink and let her neck fall back on the girl's soft fingertips. She muttered something under her breath as the pressure increased and Trish began to gently massage the back of her scalp. She let the knife slip to the floor.

The two women didn't notice the clang. The whole world rested on the pressure of fingertips. Josey closed her eyes as Trish brought her other hand into play and pressed with force. After a few minutes Josey shifted ever so slightly, away, and Trish withdrew her hands.

Josey turned around to face her masseuse. With a shy and pretty smile Trish leaned forward, near a cliff-like edge but without a care. Josey was there too. She reached for Trish's hands and stared at them, then motioned towards the table. She placed one of Trish's hands in hot oil and then did something she'd never done. She gave a manicure in reverse. She oiled, clipped, and lotioned the hands. She then cut the nails even shorter than they were originally. Trish's hands were left clean, perfect, and without chemical, paint, or product. Trish gave Josey a growing smile as she worked.

When she was finished, their eyes met.

"Do you want to stay here tonight?" Josey heard herself say.

"Yes, I do," Trish replied.

Josey, for once, felt in control. She decided to play hard. Her eyes went cold. Standing up, she looked down at Trish and ordered the girl to strip. Trish did not look surprised by the sudden change in atmosphere. She stood up and unzipped the tight purple lycra, unleashing pretty, dark breasts. Josey felt a pang of arousal.

"Take it all off," Josey ordered coolly. Trish peeled off the skirt and stood unwaveringly beautiful in a barely-there thong. Josey stared her down, taking her time looking over the fearless woman.

Josey sat down in a chair and motioned to Trish to come closer. Her touch started light. The graze of her fingers stiffened Trish's stomach and spine. Her touch roughened. She placed two hands on the girl's narrow hips and yanked her closer. Placing her nose between Trish's legs, she smelled the dripping, delicious pussy.

While she looked directly into Trish's eyes she pushed the black thong to one side and slipped a single finger in, the penetration exquisite in its slowness. A moan escaped the girl's lips.

"Turn around," Josey demanded. Trish turned slowly. Josey's fingers gripped hard, remaining inside Trish as she shifted, achingly slowly. Each movement brought a new sensation to Trish's interior walls. Trish's moaning became louder. Clutching her body forward, Josey leaned into Trish and felt the moisture thicken between her legs.

Josey felt the girl's blushing and tense body tremble with desire. Josey knew that Trish needed release but Josey wouldn't allow it. Her grip stiffened and she began to push into Trish's pulsing clit with hard knuckles. The young woman could barely hold on. Josey kept her safely on the edge.

Leaning down and pushing forward, she bit hard into Trish's back. The girl slammed against the kitchen counter. Josey knew that must have hurt, but Trish showed no sign of alarm. She continued, working a fist into Trish from behind. She clutched her hot, contracting muscles.

Trish's naked body pummeled the counter. Her whimpers became screams and then shrieks. Josey's arm was erect and unrelenting. Her other arm supported Trish's heaving torso and her fingers wrapped around Trish's open, hot mouth.

Trish became silent as her body was flooded with a stiffness that demanded release. Josey softly kissed Trish's hot neck and told her to come. Trish's body tightened and turned beet red as she released a white fluid that ran down Josey's arm. One after another her spasms slowly receded. After what seemed hours of pure ecstasy, Josey removed her cramping hand to lightly massage the woman's purpling thighs.

Josey was catching her breath when Trish fell to the ground. The breathless girl knelt before her, undoing Josey's khakis and exposing her white panties. A flash of fear struck Josey, fear that Trish would find her juices smelled bad, or worse, unwomanly.

Trish noticed Josey's body become rigid as she moved closer to taste her pussy. Instead of pausing, Trish placed her tongue squarely in Josey's overwhelmingly wet labia.

Every touch of her tongue felt like a promise. Trish drank from her like the women in the film drank from one another. Josey laid her head back and felt home rush in all around her. She let her eyes close as Trish opened her release valves and drank her pressures.

×

"Oh no! Did you cut yourself?" Josey pointed to Trish's left leg. It was all Josey could do to not mother the pretty young woman before her moving languidly in an old t-shirt and skinny jeans. Trish looked down at the maroon liquid snake lacing her calf. "It's nothing," she replied as she set down a large laundry basket full of what looked like recyclables.

The women had become inseparable since their manicured affair. It all came with such ease that they barely noticed what was happening. When Trish's parents kicked her out, Josey begged her to move into the spacious summer home. Together they fell into a quiet rhythm. The routine played out into roles that mimicked husbands, wives, siblings, or co-workers. But mostly they were collaborators and lovers.

They saw life through a similar lens. The lens was lavender in color and highlighted the tension between what was said and what wasn't. They each appreciated words and the spaces between them. Enjoying silence, their conversations were like Quaker meetings. They worked well in proximity to one another and this was the key to their happiness.

Trish bit into a large peach, juicing her right palm and chin. Josey smiled and kissed her cheek clean. One of the movers took note of the intimate play between the two women and quickly looked away with erect pupils. This annoyed Trish and her eyes slanted towards the ground in growing anger. Josey quickly placed a hand on Trish's hip and brought her close as the mover exited through the doorway.

"Thanks for staying with me. I can't imagine my mornings without you."

"Thanks for having me. It's pretty wonderful having breakfast in bed every day."

Josey pulled in for a kiss. "Don't ever leave."

"Be careful what you wish for…" Trish backed away for a moment. "Hey, are you sure everything's cool?"

Josey looked away for a split second. "I'm sure. Everything and everyone, including myself, is cool. But you're the coolest." Josey pulled her back in and kissed her softly. She didn't like to talk about her other life, avoiding the subject as much as possible. Josey knew that her refusal was a wall between them, but she just didn't feel ready. It wasn't Trish that made her feel unsafe to share. It was her own inability to know what she wanted.

She was completely high off Trish, but she kept wondering, was it Trish or the newness of the situation? Was it only hot and fun because she was away from the real world? She didn't trust herself to know what was best. But it was strange, how confident she felt with her new lover.

Confidence was a new feeling, and she didn't trust that either.

Trish impressed Josey with her fearlessness. She was ageless in her optimism. She never shied away from the truth of any given situation and she didn't sugarcoat a thing, other than Josey.

Trish touched and hungered and ate Josey like she was the last strawberry on earth. Josey suspected that they each felt a certain amount of anticipation and surprise and that that's what made it work. They didn't rely on external value or stereotypes to gauge their shared heat. They were just Hot. Moving away from her thoughts, she shifted subjects: "Want to make popcorn later?"

'Making popcorn' was code for

watching porn, and it almost always ended in a steamy session somewhere around the house. Josey had some new ideas she wanted to try out. "How 'bout Kettle Corn tonight?"

"Whatever you want, I'm game." Trish said, showing that famous half smile.

×

One by one Josey extinguished the blue pool lights. She was nude save a white hip-strung apron. Her hair was swept up in a high ponytail. She stood coolly facing Trish.

It was dusk. The light was a deep purple playing off silvery forest skins. Trish sat fully clothed in a lawn chair, staring at Josey's golden toned breasts. They both inhaled lightly as they anticipated the play about to unfold.

"Can I get you a drink, sir?" Josey asked politely.

Trish responded in a light southern accent, "Sure, honey. I'll take a bourbon on the rocks and some of your pretty pussy."

Josey walked past Trish and into the house. Trish kept her eyes on Josey's long legs and tight ass. Her loose ponytail gently bobbed. Trish wanted to pull it. Her mouth watered. Her nerves felt sharp.

Appearing moments later with a tumbler of bourbon on ice, set on a sleek red tray, Josey approached. Taking her time, she dipped her big toe into the pool. The drink spilled onto Josey's bare stomach. She dipped her finger into the drop and smoothed it along her breast, up to her bottom lip. Trish watched without moving. Silence became their lust-filled contract.

Josey's hand returned to the glass, dowsing a few fingertips into the gold syrup. The hand that she was moving along her hip and thighs disappeared beneath the front of her apron.

Trish had no view. Her nerves bristled.

Josey looked directly at Trish. "May I touch myself, please?"

"Yes, you may."

Josey balanced the tray with one hand while the other stroked her pussy. Born of a seashell, Josey's posture took on *contrapposto*. Her head leaned back, hips swaying gently, eyes closed.

The women listened to the subtle sounds of Josey's wet finger-play mimicking the lather of the pool and succulent moisture of the forest. Trish barely breathed as Josey's sounds became louder. As she fingered herself, her brow began to furrow; her muscles took on a new tension. The drink slid to one side, the tray began to dip.

Just before the drink fell from the tray and the sun behind tree line, Trish, like a perfect gentleman, rescued the glass and set it on concrete. She stayed bent before Josey, inhaling the woman's lilac scent.

Under Josey's erotic spell, Trish closed her eyes and stopped her internal monologue. She stopped editing. She relaxed her trained senses and allowed

Josey to take control. She no longer cared how things would look to other people and she no longer wanted to control how Josey saw her. She had to let go someday, and in that moment, kneeling before Venus in an apron, it seemed like a perfect opportunity to do so.

Trish watched the apron's cool white surface ruffle up in flashes of red and pink just inches from her face. Her breasts were swollen. She felt a growing need to touch Josey's trembling thighs. Her mouth skimmed the inside of a leg. Josey tasted warm and salty. Trish's lips became a snake that lived in Josey's pores. She would eat the entire leg in one gulp, first skinning the surface with her saliva. She bit in and closed her eyes, feeling the older woman's quakes and shivers through her own lips.

Trish lifted the apron and found Josey's swollen clit. Her tongue sucked in ocean-rhythm, fighting for space among Josey's slippery fingers. Trish felt a hand grab the back of her head and she moaned inside of Josey's hunger.

Trish succumbed and let Venus tell her what to do. Her mouth responded to the writhing movements. Her palms grabbed at Josey's plump ass, pulling her deeper into her mouth. Trish couldn't control anything anymore. She spanked Josey's ass hard as she pushed her tongue and teeth as deep as possible. She gave in to it all. Trish wanted nothing more than to give everything she was and could be to this woman, this goddess at the tip of her tongue.

With the sun and drink and Venus in arms, Trish quit her job.

×

She hadn't known much about what she wanted until she gave in to giving. It felt great. She was excited to begin this new life that included Josey, but for the first time Trish didn't know what to expect. Trish had had some young lovers, a few flings here and there, but nothing in comparison to how she felt when she was with Josey.

The sight of Josey, and the ease and laughter they shared, led her into new emotional territory. It wasn't that she trusted Josey, it was that she had no way to not trust her; she was defenseless. It was a double bind of sorts, and this is what Trish imagined love to be. She couldn't stand the thought of not being near Josey. She felt happy and safe when they were together.

And it was together that they shared a lust for life. They talked about everything: art, film, music, poetry, death. And sex. They spoke, ate, drank, and slept sex. Together they constructed a new body language that only they knew, and it revolved around their most intimate spaces. Trish felt confident about their relationship because there was no reason not to.

Trish knew that Josey was going through some things that were hard for her to understand. She also knew that Josey was married, and an artist, with a whole other life in New York. She felt she had no right to expect promises or commitments, but at the same time couldn't help but dream of a home with Josey in it. She hoped that Josey would eventually open up to her about her life in New York. She had no choice but to hope, because otherwise she knew she'd lose Josey. It seemed that just when Trish began to have an awareness of this fact, their love began to slip like a stone across the lake.

×

About two weeks after she moved in, Trish felt a change in temperature. Fall was edging in and Josey had become abnormally quiet. Trish noticed that Josey was spending a lot of time in the bathroom. At first she thought it was the regular ritual night bleedings, until she realized that Josey had begun making drawings in the tub. Trish figured she missed her art. She casually brought up the question one night over dinner.

Josey stared squarely into Trish's face. "I'm glad you brought this up." She said it like a challenge. "I've been meaning to talk to you about something...I was offered a show at MoMA in New York... my paintings are selling okay but I need to do a museum show to get to the next level."

"That's great! Congratulations."

"Thanks," she said coolly, looking away. "I need to go back to New York."

Trish looked down. "When?"

"Soon. Tomorrow."

"What? Tomorrow?" Trish looked away, afraid of what Josey was about to say.

"Yes, but don't worry; you can stay here as long as you like. Ryan said it was fine. I need to go deal with things…with my life." She paused. She breathed. "This time…" She looked down and began again. "This time with you has been incredible. I have felt so much with you, a freedom in my body, in my mind—that I've never felt before, and it scares me, Trish, because every time I'm with you I feel farther away from myself, or who

I think I am. And it's really confusing, because I *know* myself. I've grown used to life's disappointments, and I know from years of painful experience that love like this doesn't last, and you're making me think it can."

Josey stopped speaking and looked out the window. "The truth is, Trish, I've painted a lot longer than I've known you, or anyone... and you're so young...you can't know..." She trailed off, her eyes becoming dry and hard. "I need to do this, for my work, for me. I still want you in my life..." She trailed off again, this time to absolutely nowhere.

Josey looked across the table at her wounded lover. Trish's high cheekbones fell. Crushed, her eyes sank deep into her skull, narrowed. Venom filled her throat. Trish looked ready to spit. Her whole body caved in at the older woman's terrible words. It was all Josey could do not to take it all back, because she knew better than anyone that once hurt had set its building blocks it was impossible to undo the damage.

Trish stood up from the table. Her body shifted stiffly. Everything that was once soft had been replaced with stone. Trish returned to pain. "So that's it. You're leaving. Tomorrow." Silence, and then looking up with a dense glare, "Josey. You are selfish," Trish took a deep breath, "and until now I had given you the benefit of the doubt, because you're going through a hard time with whatever-the-fuck other life you have been ignoring for months now.

"You clearly have been on more of a vacation than I realized. You are vacant to yourself." Trish heard her own voice getting louder, with an anger that she didn't even recognize. "You can throw me away, but it will only lead to more of the same. I may be younger and dumber, but I allowed you to change me and now to hurt me. You put on a good show, Jose. I had no idea you were such a coward." Without a last look, Trish strode out the door, straddled her Vespa, and took off.

Josey was on autopilot. She had things to do. She had to shut off. Feelings would not help her now. She had to focus. She had to stretch a new canvas. A new life.

She figured Trish would be upset but hadn't thought she'd be volatile.

She laid out the facts—*they'd only been sleeping together a couple of months and Trish was so young, with her whole life ahead of her, how could she expect anything or even want anything serious?* Josey took a deep breath and got in the tub. She felt empty and let pain move her inside-out.

Josey was bloodless that night. She had to make her own marks. Gripping a razor she sliced two long lines across her right thigh. As she watched the blood seep into the hot bath water, Josey felt nothing.

Josey woke up an hour later to the sound of crying. For a quiet moment she didn't know where she was, thought she was in her bathtub in Brooklyn, and that the sounds were from the apartment next door. It took a full second to realize that she was in a cabin and that she had broken a beautiful woman's heart that night.

But who was crying? Had Trish come back? It wasn't until she looked in the bathroom mirror at a puffy wet face that she realized it was her own muffled voice that woke her. Sobs in a drowning sleep.

Where are you? I'm sorry.

×

Trish knew how to deal. She went to the nearest bar and found a half-drunk half-dead man. She dragged the zombie out back. He was almost handsome, and hungry for flesh. His breath stank of gin as he raked her neck with his bleeding gums. His rotting spine barely kept him upright. She undid his zipper. His cock was surprisingly youthful, plump and ready.

She turned around and directed his fifth limb between her ass cheeks. She impaled herself on his appetite. She held on to the chain link fence as he ripped her in two.

She and the dead man became puppets for the life they consumed but had never had. They held one another in death's grip, because disappointment was also something to feel.

He spit violently onto her back and rubbed her neck with a slick hand. He held her in a chokehold. Her breath staggered. She felt herself become purple and red as he fucked her. She liked it rough. She wanted it rougher.

Denying her death, he pulled out and rubbed his cock against her wet thighs. She was soaked. He fell to his knees to drink from her. She let it out. A black bile filled his lungs. She squirted rage into his gaping zombie hole. He drank hate like a gentleman sips lemonade. They were strangers and they were each alone as they came.

Trish may have heard the muffled buzz that announced a new text message, but she didn't stop to check. She never thought twice about going back. She would kill Josey, and the love they shared, that night.

And just like that Trish returned to porn.

Part Two
New York Doesn't Know

She stepped off the bustling platform and onto the packed subway car. It was too hot for September. The L train turned into a swampy freezer. People smelled like hot desperation. Josey never grew tired of the scent. She enjoyed watching women develop nonchalant strategies to cover their brightly lit skin. Her breasts tingled as she eyed the pretty bobbing chests and moist necklines. Josey was at the end of summer and felt happy to be home. Her body told her so.

After her return, Asher had been on his best behavior. He was proud of his wife, happy to have her back. He declared his love to her frequently, often speaking in the third person to do so. He admitted to Josey that he loved her more than his own life, that he was impossibly happy waking up next to her every morning, and that he had missed her when she was gone.

Josey enjoyed the rare attentions and met Asher with growing warmth. They settled into an old routine. Asher and Josey had been together fifteen years and their physical relationship had become nonexistent. They had become more like two people sharing an out of body experience, connected by the single silver cord known as Tax Breaks. They were best friends and lived in parallel.

They didn't need drama to remind them that they were important to one another. At least Josey didn't think they did. She'd take care of her own needs as they made themselves known. Sometimes she questioned if she was a fool to think that two people could live together, in this way, forever. *Maybe*, she thought, *but maybe not.*

She'd never cheated on her husband before and felt a strange alienation from him that gave her a high she knew came from the taboo. They'd known each other so well that she didn't even feel guilty for cheating. She felt that he would understand, because he loved her unconditionally. Therefore she felt no need to tell him anything. What happened to her simply belonged to her.

Her body also felt different since her return. The bleeding ebbed and she felt life without a monthly period in a new way. She didn't need it anymore. Her sentences became paragraphs—no stops, no pauses, no reminders of fertility. Although her thermometer was broken, she felt fresh and warm in this new state. She was refreshingly mortal and the only thing she sometimes missed, in this new life, was the long, lean body belonging to Trish. And with this mortality she changed her palette from red to blue. A color that was pre-oxygen, and pre-lingual.

The show at MoMA was called *Women Who Love Too Much*. Josey was ready, dressed in a perfect shade of red. Her hair was low-lit and her eyebrows threaded. She had made it. Her proud husband was at her side as she greeted all the men and women from her past and present.

"Oh my God, Josey. You must be so excited! You've finally arrived, after all these years!"

"Good for you!"

"You deserve this more than anyone! What's next?"

"There's so much work! Poor Asher must have been sooooooo lonely!"

"Your husband is so handsome, so

wonderful, you're so lucky."

"Your gallerist has really done wonders for you, Jo. We should do something for him. Let's send him something tomorrow!"

Voices of support streamed in around her. She didn't care that most of the comments were in some way passive aggressive and full of sordid envy. She was thrilled. The night was perfect and her work glistened like sapphires. Things felt whole and complete in a way Josey had only read about. Her life had become images from *Artforum*'s "Scene & Herd."

Josey eyed her best friend working the room. Ryan looked great in an expensive tux. Making his way over, he laid a warm and loving arm around her waist and made a dirty joke about the pool boy. Ryan knew all her secrets. She laughed casually and repressed the thread of thoughts leading to her one true love, the love of her life, Trish.

She couldn't help but think of Trish when she looked at her paintings. They were drenched in a moody pool color, feminine figures pushing at the canvas' surface. Josey knew that they were her best work, that they were all portraits of Trish. That it was her love for her that made them strong.

The women in the paintings had a strength that went beyond their materiality. With oversized toes and painted nails, they struggled against their frames, pushing thick thighs to the side, kicking edges, peeling skins. They clawed

and scratched in sexate frenzies.

They ate invisible fruits and sucked invisible strands of honey with pushed out and puffy lips. Their mouths wore money signs because they named their own value. They ate like they looked like they fucked, in a deep blue ocean's heat.

She watched the women dance around her in a sea storm. The lack was gone. There was only abundance, of body, of liquid, of saturated everything. Each canvas wore a lake and each painting was a siren that sang a silent song only the ears of a loved one could hear.

When the *New York Times* journalist asked her who her muse had been, Josey's response was to turn a deep shade of eggplant and clam up. Trish was her secret and no one, not even the art world, would take that from her. She felt protective of Trish, as if she were her own sister, daughter, or even as if she were a younger version of Josey herself. What the world got to see was just a fragment of the love she felt for Trish. She loved her even more when she was away from her.

Things felt good, until the week before her show closed. *Artforum* wrote a negative review and her gallerist still hadn't sold a thing. *They're just too lesbian…too blue…too sexy…not sexy enough…not queer enough…*

"Things will be okay, babe." Asher was doing his best to make her feel better, but Josey was inconsolable. She had shown the world her deepest secret, and in return the world slapped her in the face.

"Nothing is okay, Ash. Nothing has been okay for some time now," she barked back.

"What is that supposed to mean?" he said in a near whisper.

She looked at Asher, who seemed genuinely confused. *But how could he know?* she thought bitterly. She never told him anything; he was too busy with himself. She stared into his bright brown eyes. His handsome face had only gotten more so with age.

She remembered when they met, on the street outside of a house party in Bushwick. He had just broken up with his girlfriend and Josey was on one of her routine binges, the goal being to kill something deep inside of herself. He was candid and hilarious and called her out on the futility of her self-destructive behavior.

"How long have you been at it?" he had asked her cryptically.

Cryptic questions were Josey's specialty. "Long enough. Besides, anything worth doing is worth doing slowly." She looked away, bored.

"You don't strike me as the kind of woman who waits around long enough to know the effect you have on others, least of all yourself," he retorted. She stopped and gave him a wry look.

"You're a lawyer, aren't you?"

"If you're on the case, I certainly am." She smiled and he shot back with a grin.

That night Asher had told her who

she was, and she needed that. She needed someone to steal her from herself. Being a public defense attorney, Asher knew how to feed a mouth that bites. He wrapped his arms around her and took her home to give her a long, hot bath.

Lost in memory, Josey felt overwhelmed with love for her husband, but she also felt something else. She felt intense guilt and pity—but not for him. She felt it for herself. All these years she was lying about who she was and how she could give. She needed to be with Asher because she was afraid to be alone.

"What do you mean, Josey?" This time his voice was tense and his eyes were dark, ominous and red with clouds. In the following moments Josey confessed everything to her husband. The right secrets spilled in the wrong way, and far too late.

When Asher found out about the extent of her feelings for Trish, not to mention all the other members of Josey's lustful play, he finally began to understand how much he didn't know about his wife. He was even cheated out of a broken heart, as he realized that what he thought he had lost, he never actually had in the first place.

He walked up to her and placed his frowning lips on her pretty mouth for the last time. Gently placing a hand behind her head, he let their foreheads touch in a gesture of calmness and care. Josey took a breath and closed her eyes. He then stated in the coolest of tones, "Your self-destruction is boring me to death, Josey. I can't save you." These were his last words.

After Asher left, Josey cried non-stop for two weeks. When the flood subsided, her sadness turned into anger and then a logical self-hatred took hold, moving into a kind of self-pity that looked like wet cereal for dinner. What Josey couldn't prepare for was how intensely and utterly free she would soon feel. For the first time in a long time, Josey was alone.

And in this loneliness, feelings of responsibility washed over her, but she was without the ability to respond. She sat in her studio with the sound of a broken fan, surrounded by all the paintings of Trish that had seemed so promising just six months before. Josey realized that she missed the person. That she never should have left Trish.

She tried to remember how she'd gotten from A to B in a matter of one year. She remembered the blood. She wanted it back. She missed those murderous dreams and blank red screens. Josey realized that, ironically, she'd never even told Asher about the blood, one of the signs that marked this time in her life. But then again, she thought to herself, everyone seemed to sense it, even him. From this and certain emergency room experiences Josey deduced that people generally preferred bleeding people to leave the room.

She was appointed adjunct professor at the School of Visual Arts in Manhattan and kept on painting. Her routine was quiet and unfeeling. She was tired but couldn't sleep. Her anxiety morphed into a constant state of emergency. Her eyes settled back into her skull. Her shoulders fell. She became thinner. Sometimes she believed she was getting smaller so that she could get closer to the sky. She had a new face, one that was both younger and older than her original mask. And her paintings showed it too. The brushstrokes had flattened, and the women she made stared straight into a mirror, into themselves. Her color palette changed. Josey no longer used red or blue; she didn't need them. All she could see was black.

I still think about you.

Part Three
We At Last

"Here," the low voice admitted itself to an uncaring crowd.

She couldn't believe her ears. *That voice*, she knew without a doubt, belonged to her long lost past. She looked at the name again. "Patricia Martin?" she repeated, looking up into the spotlit classroom. Fifty-nine faces peered back.

One refused. Trish looked directly at the wall as she answered roll call for a second time: "Yeah."

Josey delivered the rest of her introduction to the class in quiet shock. She spoke at fever pitch, as if she were giving the last message to the last person on earth. She spoke desperately hoping that Trish would hear her regret, the total emotion that lived inside her.

It had been seven years since Josey saw Trish. Seven years since Trish had fled into the night on her Vespa. Seven years since Josey had lost her one true love. Her face began to swell and redden under PowerPoint transitions as she thought about their poolside affairs. She kept her eyes down, grateful that the room was dark. She knew that by now she looked old, or worse, felt old, old and humiliated.

After class, the seat was empty.

That night Josey had a message waiting in her inbox. It was cryptic and aloof. Just like Trish.

Hey Jo, I didn't know you taught. You changed your name too. Maybe we can catch a flick after class sometime. -T

www.patriciaherrerafilms.org

Josey clicked on the link. It opened to several movie trailers. Some of the films Josey recognized. She'd seen them screened during feminist film night at the university. They were film shorts, full of twisted sex scenarios, and all made by Trish. At the time Josey hadn't recognized Trish as the director, because just like

Josey, Trish had also changed her name. Josey suspected they had different motives in doing so. Josey went back to her maiden name, her mother's last name, after the divorce went through. Trish was younger, and who knows, *married?*

The films were great and Josey was very impressed with Trish's recent accomplishments. *Why was she in her class? Did she really not know Josey would be teaching it?* It was all crazy and Josey had to get to the bottom of it, for better or worse. She switched to SMS.

So nice to hear from you. I'd love to catch up. Café Loup tomorrow? Sent.

Buzzzzzz. *I'll be there. Will you be wearing that black skirt again?*

Josey smiled to herself. *I'll be wearing*

a white apron and whiskey-flavored lip gloss.
Are your lips chapped? It's cold outside.

My lips are wet and my fingers are
dripping blue hues. This keyboard won't
survive the flood.

Trish had turned it up a notch.

Good thing my hands are weatherproof.
Do you still give orders as well as I remember?

Depends on the grade. See you at the bar,
Professor. Bring your laptop.

That night Josey dreamt in an aquamarine
haze, images of water and women fluttering
over her loosely bound eyelids:

The Vespa vibrated between her thighs
and she squeezed the body that drove her
into the hot night. The woman's hair smelled
like honey and almonds. She leaned into her
neck; it was stiff and cool to the touch. They

rode facing the future, desirous of its darkness. They somehow knew where the road led. They just needed to keep steady, to believe that their desire would last, that they were worth it. Josey felt the Vespa begin to float on loose gravel. No. The bike wouldn't skid this time. She wouldn't let that happen. She tightened her hold on the machine with her thighs. The driver continued to speed steadily forward. Josey had to hold it together. She had to.

She woke feeling a soft pull between her legs. She had come in her sleep and her cotton panties were soaked. She half expected the bed to be covered in blood, but her juices were milky and held a fresh scent of spring blossoms.

She decided not to shower and threw on a black sweater-dress that hung closely to her curves. She let her hair go unwashed and loose, streaked with soft grease. She left her panties at home that day, and removed all proof of a manicure before sauntering to school like a kitten to fresh milk.

Josey lectured languidly. She let her eyes swoop over the crowd. She was careful not to focus on the dark haired beauty in the first row glaring at her. She moved with steady assurance. She felt good; she was ready to meet her match, finally.

Trish was wearing all denim, her hair cut short. She wore loads of eye make-up. Josey sensed her smirking throughout the entire class period.

Josey had to keep herself from calling on her for answers. She wanted to hear that voice again. She wanted to stare her down as she attempted to answer. She wanted to play.

Josey had never slept with a student before and had no tolerance for what she deemed an abuse of power. Now she felt that same power surging over the crowd. The class was under her electric spell. Josey was an erotic master teaching her disciples how to come in the longest and most intense possible way. Like teachers of ancient Greece, she begged for their pulsating youth. She was in charge and needed to keep the scene bloody. Everyone was welcome. *Teaching is erotic*, she thought. How boring of her to backhand its possibility into a hole in the ground, as if it were all just *wrong*.

She'd contemplated teaching in safe spaces and how people used one another, but she never considered how love could bridge those fundamental learning gaps. It was true that Josey had never had a student that didn't love her, but Trish was a special student, and the taboo only added to her growing desire. She knew she risked her reputation but she decided to worry about that after she'd had Trish in every position she could imagine.

Trish glared at her teacher. Even she was shocked by the amount of rage she still felt when confronted with Josey and the horrible rejection of the past. Trish had moved on, but seeing Josey in person was hard. She knew it'd take a moment to get over this *thing* that she was feeling.

She imagined a few violent scenes that kept ending in something highly erotic. She had to face it, she just couldn't kill Josey in the end.

Josey was still sexy, even sexier than she remembered, but something had changed. Josey was more confident, serious, and the hollows of her eyes earned. They spoke to Trish of pain and loneliness and also of being *okay*. *Because that's what people do. They get okay with age.*

Trish darted out of the class and decided to walk to Loup. It was just a few minutes away and she needed that time to work out what exactly she wanted from Josey. Trish regretted the flirtatious texts she sent the previous evening and she needed to get her thoughts straight.

Trish sat at the end of the bar, her back to the door. Trish had been a regular at Café Loup for the past year and become pals with her favorite bartender, Jake.

"Hey, Jake, I'll take a bourbon on ice."

"Sure, doll. Everything okay? You need another stool?"

"Yep. Tonight I have a hot date with the past. This one nearly killed me."

"I'll make sure it's extra hard then."

"Which, the stool or the drink?"

"Both." Her famous half-smile returned.

A few minutes later Josey waltzed in like she owned the place. "Hi, Jake, hi, Dennis, hi, Arora."

"Hey, Pretty!" The owner kissed her cheek.

Jake gave Trish a sidelong look as Josey seated herself next to Trish. Trish winked and returned her gaze to Josey's reflection in the mirror behind the bar. "I'll take the same, Jake. Thanks."

Jake turned his back to them and prepared their medicine.

"Did you walk? I was going to offer you a ride, but you disappeared."

"I walked."

"So, what brings you to town?"

"I live here. Moved here about a year ago. Came to take some classes that were more to my liking." She paused and looked Josey in the face. Their eyes met. Josey could stare anyone down. Trish looked away, into her drink. "How's life with you? Did you become the famous artist you always wanted to be?"

She knew she'd touched a sore spot,

and she regretted saying it. It proved her bitterness at how things ended between them. *Whatever*, Trish thought. *She can take it.*

"Um, yeah, well no. Not really, actually. Turns out I wasn't cut out for the famous thing. Turns out I couldn't really paint anything or anyone, after I left you."

Trish nearly choked on her drink. Was this the same woman that bailed on her without any sign of emotion whatsoever? *Was she joking?* She looked up at Josey's reflection in the mirror to see if any of these thoughts rang true. Josey kept her eyes on the bar as Trish inspected her like a lie detector. It was true, Josey looked ragged in a way, and she also seemed absorbed by what she'd learned. *Humility,*

Trish thought, *works wonders*.

"Sorry to hear that. How's Asher?"

"He's gone. Left me six years ago."

"Oh. Sorry again."

"It's okay. I deserved it all. As you know."

Trish took a long swig from her glass.

"What about you, Trish? Seems like you've become a fairly well known, up and coming filmmaker in certain feminist circles. Impressive. And you changed your name."

"Yeah, I married a Martin. Figured love is as good a reason as any to change one's name. But who wants to talk about that?"

Now it was Josey's turn to choke. *Wow*, she thought to herself, *things really have changed*. She inspected Trish through the looking glass at the bar and it all checked out, as far as Josey's intuition was concerned. *Could she still throw herself at Trish as she had planned?* She decided to let the drinks decide which action felt best.

After their relationship status updates, they both eased up. Somehow they trusted one another and the topics shifted from feminism to art to documentaries to mockumentaries to everything impersonal. Everything that wouldn't, or couldn't, touch their hearts. As they talked, the women realized that they were still in love, and that their love was born from the love they felt for the world. The love they shared came from sharing itself. And each woman knew, independently from the other, that this was the greatest kind of love.

In the end the drinks did decide. As

Josey helped Trish with her jacket, she couldn't tell if it was the bourbon or the proximity to Trish that made her swoon. She needed to confess her feelings before she passed out, or worse.

"Trish. I need to tell you something. I need to tell you how much I still think about you, about us. I regret what happened. How I left, why I left, everyday. I need you…to know that. I also need you, but at the very least…I need you to know."

Trish watched Josey with a deadpan expression and said, very slowly, "Josey, I can't do this. I killed you years ago. I can't bring you back to life now."

"Please don't put me there. Don't compartmentalize me. Please. I need this. Acknowledge that there is something that only we have. That no one else could ever touch."

"Josey. Please. Let me go."

Trish stared at her for a few more seconds before turning to hail a cab.

Josey was left alone in a street that once held two. She looked down at her black flats and big feet. She knew that Trish couldn't be hers, but she needed to say it. She needed to ask. Even if it was too late.

I'm sorry I wasn't what you wanted when you needed me most.

✕

The following week Trish wasn't in class. Josey lectured from the classroom stage like a ghost. She peered out at the students from under limp hair and a broken façade. She had nothing left to give, not without Trish.

She felt newly lost. And then she got a text.

I'm upstate, at our cafe, it read. She went directly to Grand Central Station and got on the next Metro North train.

Once on the train, *Coming. Popcorn on the beach?*

Sure, I'll bring the tray.

Josey tried to nap on the train, but she was too excited. She couldn't believe what was happening. *Don't get too worked up,* she reminded herself. Trish had been very clear the other night. Maybe she wanted to clear the air some more. Josey read somewhere that 'wounds heal in the place they were made.' Maybe that's what Trish was doing. Maybe Josey just had one big rejection to look forward to when she got there. *Better to not think about it. Better to just let it happen, whatever it may be.*

Josey settled on the beach with matches, a blanket, cheese, and crackers. As she collected driftwood she heard the light engine of a Vespa. She started the fire and waited for the elusive Trish to appear.

"Nice fire," Trish said as she fell parallel to the fading horizon line. Without hesitation, she cozied up next to Josey on the blanket. "You always were good at starting fires."

"Thanks," Josey said snidely. "Lately I've been trying my hand at putting them out. It helps that I'm an old lady."

"I don't believe that for a second. Every student in that class has *Hot for Teacher* on their playlist. You even make institutional critique look good."

"I do what I can. I have to make up for looks with bravery. That's why I'm here, in fact."

"Oh yeah? You shoot to kill these days?"

"In a sense, yes. I have plans."

"Well, count me out. I know what your plans look like."

"Do you? I don't think you do, Trish. I actually don't think you have a clue what I've been through or what I've become. But it doesn't matter. Either way, you'll find out soon enough."

"Ha ha. Okay, Joe. Can't wait." She

gave a flirtatious grin. "So what brings you up here?"

Josey socked Trish in the gut with a soft fist and Trish grabbed hold of her arm, drawing her near. Their faces nearly touched. Trish leaned in and kissed her mouth softly.

They were starving for one another and their hunger dug a hole in the sand as they buffed and polished the shore. Josey's hands flew under Trish's cotton t-shirt, her perfect breasts sweaty and heaving. Trish watched as Josey's mouth sucked at her fleshy pink nipples. She sucked like a baby, letting Trish watch in agony, desperate for more.

Both of their bodies had changed significantly. Trish's breasts were softer, her nipples longer and more responsive. Her belly had loosened and she had a new scar on the lower left of her rib cage. Josey kissed the changes, hoping to taste the ways in which Trish had healed. Josey knew that her own body looked different. Her skin had loosened and her muscles had slackened, but she actually liked the way she felt in Trish's strong grip. It felt right and things were picking up speed between them.

Trish pushed Josey's face between her legs. Josey hurriedly unbuttoned the Levi's and pulled them down enough so that she could get her hand inside. She worked her fingers into Trish and increased the pressure, throttling her hard with one hand. Her palm rolled over Trish's swollen clit. Trish gasped at Josey's aggressive stroking. "I want you," she murmured. Josey knelt down and whispered into Trish's ear, "I have wanted you for seven years. Now I have you and I am going to fuck you so hard you will never breathe the same again."

Josey got into position and worked Trish's clit over with every part of her tongue. She recognized the faint smell of blood. Trish had her period. Josey delved in with renewed vigor, the sticky liquid filling her mouth. She loved this woman and desired to know all of her interiors. She imagined she looked like a she-wolf devouring its kill. She became the dripping snout with a quiet howl.

At some point Josey thought she heard voices and saw the headlights of a pick-up truck. She didn't care, nor did she stop. Nothing would stop her from giving Trish everything she had, everything she wanted.

A few shadows lurked at the parking lot's edge and she knew whoever it was had a clear view of the two of them on the shore. Josey ripped off her turtleneck, revealing sweaty breasts lit by the moon. Trish sucked on them and whimpered as Josey continued to grasp Trish's clit between her fingers.

They rolled in the sand and Josey flipped Trish so that she had her from behind. Trish sat up and Josey kissed her neck, yanking her head back as she faced the headlights of the truck, breasts erect, Josey's fist deep inside. Trish's pussy was dripping as Josey fucked her harder. Trish was begging to come, and when she did she came hard, howling at the onlookers, the moon, and to Josey, thanking her for the apology that had been so long in the making.

The two women looked gorgeous in

the silver light. Breasts and ass cheeks moving in perfect period rhythm to the end of time. No one knew them and they barely knew one another. Their concern was gone with the world at bay. They licked at the coast between their mouths and skin while waves lapped at their toes. Their nail beds yelled for more, they consumed one another. There was no more time. There was only their agreed-upon silence, their lust-filled contract and perfectly fitted envelope. They stared into the night sky and howled like wolves. They found some space there and lived it over and over again and together.

ABOUT THE AUTHOR

Cara Benedetto is a New York City based artist.
She has exhibited at Chapter NY, Night Gallery, Metro
Pictures, and MOCA Cleveland. Her writing has been
published with Area Sneaks, Qui Parle, and Halmos.
She is Assistant Professor in Print Media at
Virginia Commonwealth University.